Antonia Barber

Dancing Shoes
Into the Spotlight

Illustrated by Biz Hull

PUFFIN BOOKS

PUFFIN BOOKS

Published by the Penguin Group
Penguin Books Ltd, 27 Wrights Lane, London W8 5TZ, England
Penguin Putnam Inc., 375 Hudson Street, New York, New York 10014, USA
Penguin Books Australia Ltd, Ringwood, Victoria, Australia
Penguin Books Canada Ltd, 10 Alcorn Avenue, Toronto, Ontario, Canada M4V 3B2
Penguin Books (NZ) Ltd, 182–190 Wairau Road, Auckland 10, New Zealand

Penguin Books Ltd, Registered Offices: Harmondsworth, Middlesex, England

First published 1998
1 3 5 7 9 10 8 6 4 2

Made and printed in England by Clays Ltd, St Ives plc

British Library Cataloguing in Publication Data
A CIP catalogue record for this book is available from the British Library

ISBN 0-140-38683-1

PUFFIN BOOKS

00062

DANCING SHOES
INTO THE SPOTLIGHT

Antonia Barber was born in London and grew up in Sussex. While studying English at London University, she spent her evenings at the Royal Opera House, where her father worked, watching the ballet and meeting many famous dancers. She married a fellow student and lived in New York before settling back in England. She has three children, including a daughter who did ballet from the age of three and attended the Royal Ballet School Junior Classes at Sadler's Wells.

Her best-known books are *The Ghosts*, which was runner-up for the Carnegie Medal and was filmed as *The Amazing Mr Blunden*, and *The Mousehole Cat*.

Antonia lives in an old oast house in Kent and a little fisherman's cottage in Cornwall.

If you like dancing and making friends, you'll love

DANCING SHOES

Lucy Lambert – Lou to her friends – dreams of one day becoming a great ballerina. Find out if Lucy's dream comes true in:

DANCING SHOES: LESSONS FOR LUCY
DANCING SHOES: FRIENDS AND RIVALS
(available August 1998)
DANCING SHOES: LUCY'S NEXT STEP
(available October 1998)

And look out for more DANCING SHOES titles coming soon

Chapter One

'It's not fair!' Lou put her chin down, pushed her chair back and sulked.

Her mother raised her eyebrows and went on trying to spoon food into Charlie, who quickly moved his head sideways. The food landed on his cheek and he looked hopefully at his sister to see if she would laugh. Lou didn't even notice.

'I don't see why Emma can't come to

our school,' she said. 'I mean, she wants
to be at the same school as me, don't you,
Emma?'

Emma had finished eating and sat with
her elbows on the table and her chin in
her hands. Her wide eyes switched
anxiously from Lou to her mother and
back as they argued. She felt really guilty
because her parents were sending her to a
private school instead of to the local
school where Lou went.

Lou was her best friend. In fact, she
was her only friend, because the
Brownes had just moved into the area.
Emma had been uprooted from the neat
little house where she had grown up,
because her dad had been promoted.
They had moved to the centre of the city
to this tall, run-down house which Emma

2

had hated at first. But then she found Lou and Lou's mother and Charlie living in the basement, and Mrs Dillon, who had once been a real ballet dancer, living in the attic.

Now she loved sharing a house with other people, and it seemed to her that her old life had been very dull. It was fun to go downstairs and have a meal with the Lamberts. Lou's mother was always too busy wrestling with Charlie to notice if Emma had her elbows on the table. Her own mother had eyes like a hawk and would have said, 'Now, Emma! Elbows, dear!'

'Don't you, Emma?' repeated Lou, frowning at her crossly.

Emma jumped, opened her eyes even wider and said hastily, 'Yes . . . yes, I do!'

But she wasn't at all sure what she was agreeing with.

'She doesn't want to go to that boring girls' school and wear that silly uniform, do you, Emma?'

'No, I –' began Emma, but Jenny Lambert interrupted her.

'It's a very smart uniform,' she said, 'and it's a good school, so don't start putting it down, Lou. Emma's parents want her to go there and that's the end of it.'

'But what's wrong with my school?' demanded Lou. 'Isn't mine a good school?'

'Yours is a very good school,' said her mother patiently as she wiped bits of food from Charlie's face, 'but Mr and Mrs Browne prefer the other one.'

'My mum doesn't mind,' said Emma.
'It's my dad . . . well, it's my granny
really. She sent my dad to a private
school, so she thinks they are better.'

'Well, they're not!' said Lou loudly.

'*I* didn't say they *were*,' protested
Emma. 'I just said that my gran . . .' She
felt close to tears. It was the first time she
had quarrelled with Lou . . .

'Now stop it, the pair of you!' Jenny Lambert broke in. She smiled at the two girls. 'Look,' she said, 'there are good and bad private schools, and there are good and bad state schools. Luckily you will both be going to good ones, and it's a really silly thing to quarrel about. After all, you will both be going to the same ballet school.'

This was a cunning move. She knew that if she could switch them on to the subject of ballet, the argument would end. Ballet was the strong bond that tied the two girls together, and they were both starting at the Maple School of Ballet as soon as the term began. There had been a bad time when it seemed that Emma would start without Lou. Jenny Lambert was a widow and she couldn't afford

Lou's ballet lessons yet. But Mrs Dillon, who lived upstairs, had once danced with the famous Russian Bolshoi Company. She had persuaded the owner of the ballet school, Miss Maple, to give Lou free lessons for a year.

Every time Lou thought about it, she felt a thrill of excitement which started in the pit of her stomach and ended up making her ears glow. She sometimes thought people would actually be able to see them glowing, if they were not hidden under her mop of hair. She smiled at the thought and Emma smiled too, with relief. The two girls got down from the table and went out together to play in the garden.

But that night, when her mother had kissed her 'Good night' and turned to leave, Lou said suddenly, 'Lots of the girls at the ballet class come from Emma's new school . . . I've seen them going in . . . in their uniforms. She'll know them all . . . and I won't . . . and then one of them will be her best

friend . . . and I'll be left out!' It was a wail of despair.

Her mother sat on the bed; she hugged Lou and wiped her eyes. 'Emma is your friend,' she said gently. 'She really likes you a lot and, after all, you do almost live together.'

Lou sniffled and snuffled.

'Trust me,' said her mother. 'It will be all right.'

Chapter Two

The changing room at the Maple School
of Ballet was packed with little girls
undressing. The bigger ones, like Lou
and Emma, had come straight from
school by themselves or had been
dropped off by parents in cars. The
smaller ones had been brought by
mothers or au pairs.

The younger ones were making a lot of
noise and confusion. Skirts were being

unbuttoned and jumpers pulled over heads and small bodies squeezed into stretchy, pale blue leotards. Hair was being brushed and pulled back into proper ballerina style. All this caused loud squeaks of protest and sometimes a howl of anguish as hasty hands pulled the wrong way.

The older girls were gathered in a group at one end of the room. They talked in lowered tones to make it quite clear that they were not part of the squeaking mass. Quite a few were hanging up the striped blazers and pleated skirts of Emma's school; others wore a uniform Lou did not recognize. None of them shared her flared grey skirt and the blue sweatshirt with the local school's logo. All the girls seemed to know each other,

11

even those who came from different schools. Emma said, 'Hello!' eagerly to a girl who was in her class. The girl paused, in the middle of tying back long, blonde hair and said, 'Oh . . . hi!' in a bored voice. Then she looked away and began to talk to another girl.

Emma went pink and turned back to Lou. Lou tried not to feel pleased. She knew it was mean, but she was so afraid that Emma would become part of a group from which she would be left out. She gave Emma a big smile. Emma's pink face smiled back and faded to its usual colour.

Lou pulled up her tights, wriggled into her leotard and felt magic. She felt like a real ballet dancer. She longed to prance and leap about like the little ones, but she could see that it was not the thing if you were in the older class. The blonde girl had fixed her hair and was standing with her hands on her hips, her weight on one leg and the other toe slightly pointed. She looked like a dancer waiting in the wings of a theatre. Lou tried to imagine herself standing just like that, bored, unsmiling and very, very superior . . . but it was no use. She could only see herself madly leaping and twirling upon a brightly lit stage.

'Shall I do your hair?' asked Emma.

They had practised this over and over at home; Emma had learned how to do it at the ballet school's Beginners' Workshop. Lou scooped back her thick, dark hair and twisted it into a knot. Emma stuck in the hairpins to hold it in

13

place and fixed a little blue bun-net over it. Then Lou did the same for Emma's pale, smooth hair. This left only their shoes. Lou had hoped for satin shoes with ribbons that crisscrossed about the ankle, but the younger classes wore plain leather ballet shoes with bands of elastic. At least it made them easy to put on.

When they were ready, they looked up and found to their dismay that the older girls had disappeared.

'Quick!' said Lou. 'We don't want to turn up when the lesson has started!'

Panicking, they scrambled through the crowd and out into the quiet echoing hallway. They hurried across the polished floor to where voices came from a half-opened door. This led into a studio with mirror glass covering one wall and a wooden *barre* at which half a dozen girls stood doing *pliés* to warm up. The others were scattered about the room in various positions.

They turned as Lou and Emma came in and seemed surprised to see them. The blonde girl said something in a low voice and several of the others giggled.

Luckily, at that moment a tall, elegant woman swept into the room and said, 'Good afternoon, girls.'

An answering chorus said, 'Good afternoon, Mrs Dennison.'

'Find your spaces.'

The girls took up spaces around the room. Lou and Emma hid themselves at the back where the others wouldn't notice their efforts and snigger.

'*Révérence!*'

Twelve girls put the right foot forward, swept the left behind, raised their arms sideways and sank into an elegant curtsy with bowed heads; twelve girls rose smoothly again and stood in first position.

Lou and Emma did this beautifully as they had practised it with Mrs Dillon. Lou felt very pleased with herself. She began to wish that she had not hidden herself at the back.

Then the first blow fell. Mrs Dennison took out a list and began to call out names. The girls answered in turn, but Lou's and Emma's names were not included.

'The two girls at the back,' said Mrs Dennison, 'what are your names?'

'Lucy Lambert and Emma Browne,' said Lou.

'You are not on my list. What class are you in?'

'I think we're in Beginners,' said Emma, going pink again.

'Ah, Beginners are across the hall,' said Mrs Dennison firmly.

Lou had never been so humiliated in all her life. She went quite as pink as Emma while a ripple of laughter spread around the room. They had to walk through all the others to reach the door and it seemed to take for ever. As she passed the blonde girl, Lou saw that she was trying to hide a cat-like smile.

When the door closed behind them and they stood alone in the empty corridor, Emma looked as if she might be going to cry.

'Oh, come on, Em, cheer up!' said Lou. 'Who wants to be with that snobby lot anyway?'

But there was worse to come. When Lou finally plucked up courage and opened the door across the hall, they found to their horror that it was full of the little ones!

Chapter Three

The studio had the same *barre* and mirrored wall, but the younger ones were not standing elegantly poised like the older girls. Some were hopping on one leg, others were squirming with nervousness. Several mothers sat on chairs at one side, smiling at the antics of their children.

I don't believe this! thought Lou. They cannot be serious. They can't expect Emma and me to dance with this lot!

Then she noticed a young, slim, sweet-faced woman who stood in front of the class, smiling at them expectantly. She had smooth, dark hair and wide eyes and reminded Lou of Margot Fonteyn dancing Juliet in her favourite video.

The young woman said, 'You must be Lucy and Emma. I am Miss Ashton and we are all very pleased to see you.' She turned to the class. 'Now, girls, we are very lucky to have Lucy and Emma with us for our first term. They are going to be at the front of the class and, as they already know a little about ballet, they will help to show you how the steps should be done.'

Lou suddenly felt much better. She

glanced at Emma and saw that she too
had brightened.

The teacher made room for them at the
front and as she did so she said, 'You'll
see that we have a little audience today.
Some parents like to stay for the first
lesson, to see that their daughters settle in
happily.' Then she turned to the whole
class and said, 'First we shall learn to do
a lovely curtsy, which is called a
révérence. I wonder if Lou or Emma can
tell me why we do this. Emma?'

'It's to greet the teacher and show
respect,' said Emma in a tiny voice.

'And to thank her for giving us
priceless knowledge,' added Lou, rather
more loudly. Mrs Dillon had told her that.

Miss Ashton smiled and said that they
were quite right. 'We do the *révérence* at

the beginning and end of every lesson,'
she told them. Then she swept into a
curtsy so graceful that Lou wondered why
she wasn't dancing on a grand stage
instead of teaching at the ballet school.

The lesson was under way and soon
Miss Ashton had the twelve younger ones

standing tall and raising their arms like birds' wings. Some got carried away and flapped a lot, so Miss Ashton asked Lou and Emma to demonstrate.

Lou began to see that there were good things about being in the Beginners' class. Instead of having to hide at the back and being the worst at everything, she and Emma were the best in the class. And Miss Ashton seemed to go out of her way to make them feel important. Lou even enjoyed the audience of mothers. She would have liked to have them there every week. She felt sure that they were all admiring her gracefulness and hoping that their daughters would learn to dance as well as she did. In fact, the mothers never took their eyes from their own little darlings and each one thought hers the

star of the class, but fortunately Lou did
not know this.

The lesson was very informal. After the
little ones had all managed a rather
wobbly *révérence*, they did a lot of
moving to music. They flapped like birds,
hopped like rabbits and danced like
fairies. This was all a bit childish, and
Miss Ashton had a particular smile for
Lou and Emma which said plainly, 'Of
course, all this is really too simple for
you.' But it was great fun and Lou told
herself that she was setting a standard for
the others to aim at. Her bird flapped so
lightly, it seemed as if it might take off at
any moment. Her rabbit hopped so
convincingly, you could have fed it
lettuce. And as for her fairy . . . it was so
graceful, she felt that she could certainly

have granted three wishes, if anyone had
bothered to ask for them.

After half an hour the younger ones
went to change, but Lou and Emma
stayed behind. Miss Ashton wanted to see
how much Mrs Dillon had taught them.
They did first, second and third foot
positions with the correct *port de bras*,

which were positions of the arms. They showed her their *pliés*, holding the *barre* lightly and bending their knees gracefully down and then up again. Lastly, they did *tendus*, which meant pointing their toes to the front, side and back.

All the steps in ballet seemed to have French names. Miss Ashton said it was because the first ballet school ever had been in France, hundreds of years before.

It was exciting to see themselves reflected in the great, clear wall mirror instead of the wardrobe door mirror that they used at home.

Miss Ashton said that they were doing very well. 'I hope you don't mind spending your first term with the Beginners,' she said, 'but we thought it would be best.'

'The older ones will make fun of us,' said Emma, who knew she would have to face them at school.

'But I think it would have been worse to make mistakes in front of them,' said Miss Ashton. 'You see, they have all been dancing for about two years. But with extra coaching, we hope you will be able to join their class next term. Miss Maple tells me that you are having special lessons from a lady who once danced with the great Bolshoi Company.'

'Yes,' said Emma proudly, 'she was called Reena Brushover.' (Her real name had been Irina Barashkova, but Lou and Emma were not good at Russian.)

'But she is Mrs Dillon now,' added Lou.

'Then I think that with such good

teaching you will soon catch up.
Meanwhile –' she smiled at them –
'perhaps it would help if you finish a
little early.'

Lou and Emma could have hugged her
for understanding their problem. They
were changed and dressed in a flash, and
half-way home before the older girls
came out.

Chapter Four

'There's this blonde girl called Angela who is really horrid to me,' said Emma gloomily.

Mrs Dillon clucked sympathetically. Lou's mother had gone to her evening class, Charlie was fast asleep and the girls had just finished their ballet lesson. It was fun being taught by Mrs Dillon, but she was very strict. They had done four positions with *port de bras* and they had

to get them just right. Then they did *pliés*
and *tendus* and something new called
glissés, which were like *tendus* only you
lifted your toes off the ground. Mrs
Dillon said they had worked very hard.

Now they sat drinking milk and eating
biscuits and told Mrs Dillon all their
troubles.

'This Angela is calling you rude names?' she asked.

'Well, no . . . But whenever I walk past her and her friends at school, I always hear them giggle.' Emma squirmed at the memory.

'Pouff! This is nothing!' said Mrs Dillon. 'With some girls there is always much giggling. Now when I first joined the Bolshoi school, I had to face real insults!'

'Did you?' Emma perked up. She loved to hear Mrs Dillon talk of the days when she had been Reena Brushover.

'Mostly they were city girls,' Mrs Dillon explained, 'while I was a little country girl, from beyond the mountains, who loved to dance. My accent was different from theirs and so they taunted me, calling me "peasant".'

'Oh, wow!' said Emma. 'You were like Giselle in the ballet. She was a peasant girl who loved to dance.'

Mrs Dillon thought about this and then preened, looking very pleased with herself. 'Yes,' she said, 'I was very much like Giselle.'

Lou had always wanted to know why Mrs Dillon had left the Bolshoi. Her mother said it was for love, but she had never dared to ask. Now she said casually, 'Did you fall in love with a nobleman . . . like Giselle?' She could picture him arriving in a carriage at the stage door and sending Reena Brushover baskets of flowers.

Mrs Dillon gave a dry little laugh. 'Alas, no,' she said. 'He was young man who moved the scenery.' She thought about him with a faraway look in her eyes and added, 'But he was very handsome.'

Lou wondered where he was now. 'Did he die?' she asked, thinking of her own father.

'No,' said Mrs Dillon, in a matter-of-fact voice. 'He was running away with an actress.'

'How awful!' said Emma. 'Did you go mad? . . . Like Giselle, I mean, when Loys deceived her.'

This time Mrs Dillon laughed out loud. 'I was very cross,' she said, 'but I did not go mad. I was very happy to be in England, even without my husband.'

'Were you dancing in England?' asked Lou.

'No, I did not dance after I left the

Bolshoi . . . but I gave lessons
sometimes.'

'Why didn't you join the Royal
Ballet?' said Emma.

'I tell you the truth,' said Mrs Dillon,
lowering her voice confidentially. 'For
some time, while I danced with the
Bolshoi, I was having pain in my knee.
Soon it would show, and I would have to
leave the company. I knew I would never
travel abroad again and life in Russia was
hard. I saw my chance with this
handsome young man. Once I was
married, no one could make me leave
England . . . not even when he left me.'

'But didn't your heart break when he
went?' asked Emma. 'Giselle's heart
stopped beating.'

'Her heart was weak,' said Mrs Dillon

scornfully. 'She was French, I think. But the heart of a Russian peasant is strong; she can bear much suffering.'

'Just as well,' said Lou practically, 'or you could have ended up drifting around the forest in a long white dress.'

'Like Giselle!' added Emma.

'This is true.' Mrs Dillon nodded agreement. 'And you also must be

35

strong,' she told Emma. 'You must not let this giggling girl cause you pain. You will work hard at your dancing and then she will be the foolish one.'

Emma looked quite cheerful. 'Yes,' she said. 'I will . . . I'll work really hard . . . and then no one will be able to laugh at me.'

'WE'LL BE THE BEST,' chanted Lou. She punched the air and shouted, 'Yes!'

'Yes!' echoed Emma, following suit.

'You girls wake up Charlie,' growled Mrs Dillon, 'and I show you what real trouble is!'

Chapter Five

Lou and Emma were doing well. They were nearly half-way through the term and Miss Ashton said she felt sure they would be ready to move to the older class after Christmas. She also said that she would miss them, that it was a great help having them in the Beginners' class.

Lou and Emma loved Miss Ashton. Sometimes they felt they did not want to leave her class and join Mrs Dennison's.

Whenever they thought about it, they
remembered that long, shameful walk to
the door when she had thrown them out
without a second thought. Miss Ashton,
they agreed, would never have done that.
She always went out of her way to make
her pupils feel good. When Lou and
Emma did their 'thank you' curtsy to her,
they really meant it.

They were both very popular with the
younger ones. Miss Ashton was very kind
to her Beginners and Lou and Emma
were trying to be just like her. So they
never behaved as if they thought they
were better than the others, but cheerfully
joined in with all the skipping and
hopping and flying about. Sometimes it
was more like acting than dancing. Miss
Ashton showed them how ballet dancers

speak without words. For 'listen' you put one hand to your ear, for 'love' you clasped two hands to your heart and for 'marriage' you pointed to your ring finger.

The classes were great fun and afterwards the younger ones would crowd around them, saying, 'Lou, did you see

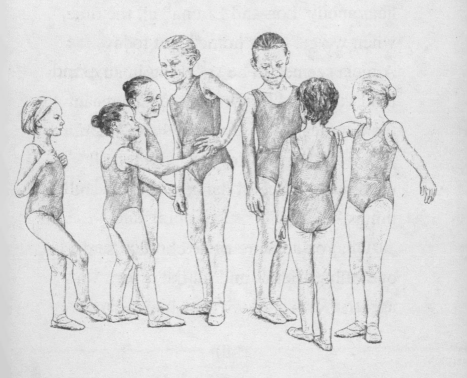

my rabbit jumps?' or 'Emma, is this how a bird goes?'

As they entered the changing room before their next lesson, the warm welcome from the younger ones helped to make up for Angela and her friends being so snooty. The mothers and au pairs had also become very friendly, saying, 'We hear about "Lou and Emma" all the time, when we get them home.' But today Angela seemed to be speaking in an extra loud voice and Lou knew that she meant them to hear. 'I'm sure it will be *Aladdin* this year,' she was saying, 'and they'll need really graceful dancers in veils and things.'

'Oh, you are sure to be chosen,' said one of her friends and all the others agreed.

Horrid little creeps! thought Lou crossly, and wondered what they were talking about. She tried to pretend she hadn't heard them, and she and Emma walked off to their class with heads held high, their hands clutched by the chattering little ones.

Miss Ashton's class followed the usual pattern until they came to the last five minutes, when she announced that she had some special good news for them.

'Every Christmas', she said, 'the local dramatic society puts on a pantomime. Do you all know what a pantomime is?'

'*Cinderella*, Miss!' . . . '*Beauty and the Beast*!' . . . '*Jack and the Beanstalk*!'

It seemed that everyone knew and had been to see more than one.

'That's good . . . good . . .' Miss Ashton

hushed them all. 'The ballet school chooses dancers to take part in the show. In the past it has always been girls from the older classes, but this year, because we have Lou and Emma to help us, we have decided to let the Beginners have a turn.'

The class went wild with excitement, and Lou and Emma looked at each other with broad grins. Angela would be furious, thought Lou with real glee. She pictured herself and Emma dancing gracefully in the 'veils and things', but what would the little ones wear? They would look a bit funny in veils.

'Please, Miss Ashton, which pantomime is it?'

'Guess,' said Miss Ashton.

They guessed in turn, but each time she

shook her head. Lou thought she knew and at last called out '*Aladdin*!' But Miss Ashton shook her head again.

'Give up!' chorused the young ones.

'It's . . . *Dick Whittington and His Cat* and you are all going to be . . . the little mice. Except for Lou and Emma, that is, and they are going to be TWO BIG RATS!'

As the two girls walked home together, Lou sighed. 'Veils and things would have been nice.'

'Yes . . .' said Emma doubtfully. She couldn't picture herself in veils. 'But rats and mice will be more fun,' she pointed out. 'I mean, it will be like being in *The Nutcracker*.'

Lou hadn't thought of that. Suddenly

the rats came to life in her mind. She
knew that she would be the most rat-like
rat ever. She grinned at Emma.

'Angela and her friends are all cats,'
she said, 'but we are the rats and –' she
raised her voice – 'RATS RULE! OK?'

'OK!' shouted Emma.

They raised their hands and slapped them together. Then they ran the rest of the way home, laughing.

Chapter Six

It was Emma's birthday the next week,
but she wasn't happy.

'What can I do?' she asked Lou.
'Honestly, I wish I didn't have to have a
birthday.'

Lou was shocked. She couldn't imagine
anyone not wanting their birthday,
especially if they had rich parents like
Emma's who could buy her any present
she asked for.

'Can't you tell your mum you don't want a party?' she asked. Lou always went to her own mother when things went wrong, and Mrs Browne seemed a very kind person.

'What? Tell her I don't want one because I haven't got any friends?' said Emma bitterly. 'Tell her that Angela shuts me out at school and the other girls do what she says?'

'Well, that's not your fault,' said Lou reasonably. 'I'm sure your mum would understand.'

'No, she wouldn't,' said Emma. 'She was always very popular at school. Everyone wanted to be her friend. She thinks because I'm her daughter I ought to be the same.'

There was a long silence.

'I've got friends at my school,' said Lou, trying to be helpful. 'We could invite them and then they could be your friends too.'

'But my mum would know they were from your school, wouldn't she?'

'I suppose so.' Lou could see no practical way to kit out her school friends in striped blazers for the day. Most of her friends wouldn't be seen dead in striped blazers anyway. There was another long silence. Then Lou had a brainwave.

'Couldn't you talk to my mum about it?'

Emma brightened at once.

They were minding Charlie, so they picked him up and lugged him downstairs to where Lou's mum was wrestling with her evening-class homework.

'Can we talk to you?' asked Lou.

Her mother looked up at the two solemn faces.

'Is it urgent?' she asked. 'Because I'm pretty busy.'

'It's urgent,' said Lou.

Jenny sighed and put down her pen. 'Well, I could use a break,' she said. 'Come and talk to me while I make some coffee.'

They crowded into the tiny kitchen.

Emma sat on the stool clutching Charlie, while Lou told her mother everything. Jenny listened seriously and thought hard while she poured milk and coffee. Then she said, 'Sometimes, when children get a bit old for party games and paper hats, they have birthday outings instead to somewhere exciting. Of course, they can't take lots of friends, because it would cost too much, so they just take their best friends.'

Emma gazed up at her with admiration. 'Oh, brilliant!' she said. 'So I could ask for an outing with Lou instead of a party and my mum would never know . . .'

'We could go to the ballet,' said Lou hopefully.

'Oh, yes!' From the depths of despair, Emma was suddenly on top of the world.

'I could say I wanted to see *The Nutcracker* . . . with the mice and rats. Oh, thanks, Mrs Lambert!' She dumped Charlie on the floor and gave Jenny a sudden hug, spilling her coffee. 'Let's go and ask now,' she said to Lou.

Charlie, who quite liked an adventurous life, shrieked joyfully as he found himself flying upstairs again, clutched between

Lou and Emma. Mrs Browne was in her bedroom, winding heated rollers into her hair.

'Can we talk to you?' asked Emma breathlessly.

'Well, yes,' said Mrs Browne cautiously. 'As long as you keep Charlie away from the rollers.'

So Lou sat on the bed and played 'To market, to market, to buy a fat pig' with Charlie, while Emma told her mother her plans for the outing.

'I want to go to the Opera House and see *The Nutcracker*,' she said, 'and sit in the most expensive seats.' She thought this would make sure that she could only take Lou with her.

Mrs Browne seemed to like the idea. 'I suppose you are getting a bit old for party games,' she said, 'and you could wear your Laura Ashley dress, the one with the pink sash.' She seemed to be doing sums in her head as she unwound the rollers. 'I think', she said at last, 'that we could manage a party of five: you and me, and Lou, of course, and two of your other friends.'

Emma's face fell, but she thought fast. Then she asked, 'Can I have anyone I choose?'

'Of course,' said Mrs Browne. 'After all, it is your birthday.'

'Right,' said Emma triumphantly. 'Well, in that case I choose you and Lou, Lou's mum and Mrs Dillon!'

Chapter Seven

They had practised the dances over and
over again. The first one came near the
beginning of the pantomime. Dick
Whittington had come to London to seek
his fortune and was offered a job by a
rich merchant if his cat could get rid of a
plague of mice. The merchant had a
beautiful daughter whom Dick fell in love
with.

To their delight, the Beginners found

that this part would be played by Miss
Ashton. The merchant's daughter was
very frightened of mice, so they had to
chase her about and Miss Ashton had to
pretend to be scared. The little ones
thought it was great fun. They had to
hunch their shoulders and take tiny,
quick, mouse-like steps. They also had to

steal food from the tables and the cupboards. Then when the cat came, they dropped the food and ran away squeaking, while the merchant's daughter fainted gracefully into Dick Whittingon's arms.

Dick was played by a pretty young woman named Alison. She came to the ballet school to rehearse with them and strode about in tights, slapping her thighs. This was supposed to show that she was a boy. Lou thought it a bit odd, because none of the boys she knew ever strode about slapping their thighs. They were more inclined to slouch about and slap each other. Lou and Emma knew that the principal boys in pantomimes were always played by women and the dames by men, but no one seemed to know why.

The mice had an even better time in the second act. Dick and his cat had sailed with one of the merchant's ships to Africa, where the king had a serious rat and mouse problem. He offered Dick a fortune in gold if his cat could get rid of them. This fortune meant that Dick could marry the merchant's daughter, so of course the cat set to work and killed them all.

The children loved this, as they had to roll over and play dead with their legs stuck up in the air. The dead mice could be heard giggling as they were dragged off stage. The two rats, Lou and Emma, were the last to die. Lou did a very good stagger all over the stage before falling on her back. This made Alison laugh so much, she told Lou to keep it in.

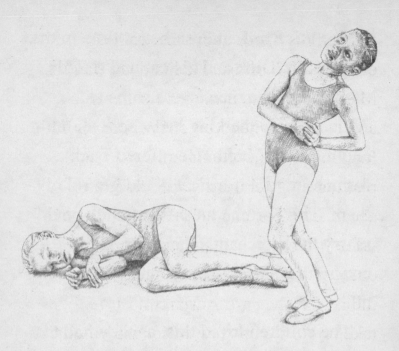

At last, the great day came when the
dancers joined the rest of the cast for a
rehearsal. Now they found themselves in
a hall with a real stage, facing rows of
empty seats. When Lou thought of the
audience sitting in those seats, she got
butterflies in her stomach.

The producer was called Adrian. He

flapped his hands about and called everybody 'darling'. He liked the dances Miss Ashton had arranged for her mice and laughed when Lou did her 'dying rat' for him. A stout older man, who was playing the Merchant, said something about 'children and animals, they'll act you off the stage if you give them half a chance', which raised a big laugh from the rest of the cast. Adrian told Lou to take no notice, as they were just jealous. Lou didn't mind anyway. It was so exciting to have an audience, even if it was only the rest of the cast. She didn't mind whether they clapped or laughed, so long as she made them do it.

When they had finished their dances, they sat in the seats and watched the others. Emma confessed to Lou that she found dancing for an audience rather scary, but Lou would not have it.

'Look,' she told Emma firmly, 'you once said your life was boring and I said it wouldn't be if you were my best friend. Right?'

'Yes,' said Emma doubtfully.

'Well, then,' said Lou. 'It's not scary, it's exciting! It's the same sort of feeling, Em, only it's good, not bad.'

'Oh,' said Emma, 'yes . . . I see . . .' She felt a lot better now that Lou had explained it.

The rehearsal went pretty well, although even the grown-ups got things wrong at times. Then Adrian would say, 'No, darlings . . . no. It's not working, is it? Let's have a little think.' Then he would change it, so that it worked better.

60

The Cat was played by a boy called Richard. He was Alison's brother and he was only fourteen. Lou liked him, but he wouldn't sit with her and Emma. She thought he was afraid of being lumped with 'the children'.

At the end of the rehearsal Adrian said, 'Well, it's coming along nicely, but we could do with a bit more business. Rack your brains, darlings, and see what you can come up with.'

'What's "business"?' Emma asked Miss Ashton as they went home.

'Well, it means little bits of action that add to the excitement or make the audience laugh,' she explained.

Lou thought this sounded very promising. She decided to dream up a bit more 'business' for the rats.

Chapter Eight

Mrs Browne had ordered a taxi to take
them all to the door of the Opera House,
so that they could arrive fresh and
beautiful. The taxi had two extra little
seats that folded down. Lou and Emma
sat on these, facing the two mothers and
Mrs Dillon. The old lady was wearing
what Lou called her 'Reena Brushover
outfit' and looked every inch the retired
ballerina.

Lou and Emma were also looking the part. Emma had a white party frock with a full skirt and a pink sash. Normally Lou would have thought it too old-fashioned, but it seemed just right for going to the ballet. She had told her mother about it, and they went down to the charity shop and found another very similar one. Lou's was also white but it had smart pink bands on the bodice and around the hem.

The traffic was getting slower as they reached the centre of the city. Lou began to worry in case they were late, but at last the taxi drew up outside a big building with pillars and arches.

'Jump out,' said Mrs Browne. 'We're holding up the traffic.'

'Why is it called the Opera House if it's for ballet?' asked Emma.

Lou's mother explained that it was used for opera as well as ballet because both needed a very big stage.

Inside it was all red and gold. They left their coats in the cloakroom and made their way up a very splendid, red-carpeted staircase. Half-way up was a landing with a huge mirror reflecting the elegant visitors as they climbed the stairs. There was a long red-velvet bench in front of the mirror and Lou wished that she could sit on it.

At the top of the staircase, they showed their tickets to a young lady who directed them along a narrow corridor. Mrs Browne checked the number on her ticket with a row of numbered doors and said, 'This must be it.'

When they passed through the door,

Lou and Emma could hardly believe their
eyes. They seemed to be in a small red
and gold room with just five gold chairs
in it. But one wall of the room was
missing; instead you could look down
from a balcony into the whole vast
theatre.

'Where are we?' asked Emma in
astonishment.

'It's called a box,' said Mrs Browne proudly, 'and it's a special treat because it's your birthday.'

Lou was staring at the great curtains that hid the stage. She knew that she had seen them before and realized, with a shock, that this was the theatre where Margot Fonteyn had danced in *Romeo and Juliet*. Those were the curtains she had seen on the video the day she first decided to learn ballet. It seemed to her that she had come to a place of pure magic, and when the curtains swept aside and *The Nutcracker* began, she knew that she was right.

The first act took place at a party with little girls wearing dresses just like their own. Lou longed to join them, to dance with them on that brightly lit stage. But

she had learned enough ballet by now to
know that, although their dancing looked
simple, it was way beyond her level.
Clara, the heroine, looked rather like
Emma, with smooth, fair hair. She was
given a present of a wooden nutcracker,
shaped like a strange little man. After the
party, she fell asleep and all the toys came
to life.

When the interval came, the two
mothers went off to get a drink, but the
girls did not want to leave the wonderful
little box. So they stayed with Mrs Dillon
and ate ice cream and admired the great
auditorium and watched the audience
come and go. There were lots of the little
boxes on both sides of the theatre and
quite a few had families with children in
them. They stared at each other and some

little children on the other side waved. Lou and Emma waved back.

'I'd like to rent this box,' said Lou with a sigh, 'and live in it for the rest of my life.'

Emma said she would live with her.

In the second act, the strange Nutcracker and the toy soldiers fought against a horde of mice led by the evil King Rat. It ended in a sword fight which made Lou think about *Dick Whittington and His Cat* and the rats. The Nutcracker turned into a handsome prince and carried Clara away to the Land of Sweets. It ended with a wonderful display of glittering costumes and brilliant dancing.

At last it was all over. Lou and Emma were so dazzled that they could not bear to leave the little box.

'Can't we stay here and watch until the last person has gone?' begged Emma hopefully.

'We need to get our coats,' said Mrs Browne, 'and there will be a long queue.'

'We'll stay here with Mrs Dillon,' said Lou, 'and then meet you on that bench half-way up the stairs.'

The mothers agreed and the girls watched from the box as the big auditorium emptied. Then they made their way to the bench on the landing. Lou had set her heart on sitting there, knowing that everyone would look at them as they came down the stairs. One elderly woman smiled as she came towards them and then paused.

'May I just say how beautifully you all danced?' she said to Lou and Emma, in a

strong American accent. Before they
could answer, she turned to Mrs Dillon.
'Are you their teacher, ma'am?' she
asked.

'I am,' said Mrs Dillon politely.

'You must be very proud of them,' said
the American lady.

'Very proud,' said Mrs Dillon.

The lady smiled again and went on down the stairs.

Open-mouthed, the two girls stared after her. At last Emma said, 'She thought we were two of the dancers . . . from the ballet.'

'Yes,' said Mrs Dillon calmly.

'Because of our old-fashioned frocks?' added Lou.

'Yes,' said Mrs Dillon again.

'And you didn't tell her that we weren't,' said Emma wonderingly.

Mrs Dillon raised her eyebrows. 'Who am I', she said, 'to destroy a dream?'

Chapter Nine

The next rehearsal was a special one for
the Rats and Mice. The costume designers
were two students from the local art
college and they had brought marvellous
heads of papier mâché for the girls to try
on. So far they had made only one of
each, to see if they fitted well and could
be worn comfortably during the dancing.

The mouse mask was rather sweet, but
the rat mask looked wicked, and Lou and

Emma couldn't wait to try it on. At first it
wobbled a bit, but Jo and Mike, the
students, worked on it until it was quite
steady. The eye-holes were a bit small,
but a few snips with the scissors soon put
that right.

'It's brilliant!' said Lou. 'It's as good as the ones in *The Nutcracker*.'

The students looked pleased, and it was true that when Lou wore it, she felt as if she was dancing on the stage of the Opera House.

She had watched the King Rat in *The Nutcracker* carefully. He had a wonderful way of twirling his whiskers, as if they were a big moustache. It made him look like a real villain. Lou tried it with the mask on and Adrian said it was 'a splendid bit of business'.

'Actually,' said Lou, 'I've got another bit of business from *The Nutcracker* –'

'What did I tell you?' interrupted the Merchant. 'Children and animals, they ought to be banned.'

'Shut up, Henry,' said Adrian, 'and let's

hear what she's got to say.'

'Well, you did ask us to dream up some bits,' said Lou indignantly.

'Take no notice of him,' said Adrian. 'He's just winding you up.'

The big man laughed and suddenly he reminded Lou of Jumbo Jones, her form teacher, who was often sarcastic but quite nice underneath. So she smiled at the Merchant and he smiled back.

'Come on, then,' said Adrian, 'let's have it.'

'Well,' said Lou, 'all the Mice and Rats getting caught . . . one after the other . . . it's a bit *samey*. But in the ballet, the King Rat and the Nutcracker fought with wooden swords . . . and I thought, maybe, Emma and I could fight with the Cat.'

'Yeah . . . great!' said Richard.

'Sounds good to me,' said Adrian. 'What about it, darling?' he turned to Miss Ashton. 'Could you arrange something? We don't want them hacking away at random and poking each other's eyes out.'

So, while the others rehearsed on stage, Miss Ashton took Richard and the two girls to the far end of the hall and they worked out the movements together.

Emma kept ducking every time Richard lunged towards her, so they agreed that the first Rat should die fairly quickly. Lou was to be a fiercer Rat and kept the Cat at bay for longer. Then, when he finally ran her through with his wooden sword, Lou did her long-drawn-out death stagger.

'My granddaughter will be sick as a parrot when she sees that.' It was the

Merchant's voice and Lou realized that he had been watching them. 'She wanted to be in the panto herself,' he added.

'Your granddaughter?' asked Emma.

'Yes,' said the Merchant. 'Name of Angela . . . Goes to your ballet class . . . Goes to your school too,' he said to Emma. 'Are you two friends?'

Emma looked embarrassed. 'Well, not really,' she said. 'I mean . . . I'm new this term . . . and she's already got friends.'

'Ah, like that, is it?' The Merchant nodded. 'Wants sorting out, that girl does. Bit of a madam at times.'

Their hearts warmed towards him.

As they went home, Emma said, 'Fancy him being Angela's grandfather! The Merchant, I mean. He's really nice, even if he does wind us up a bit.'

'Well, he would, wouldn't he?' said Lou. 'He's a Wind-up Merchant.'

Emma thought this was very witty and so did Lou. They tried it on Mrs Browne when they got home, but she didn't understand the joke. So they decided to save it for the next rehearsal and try it out on Richard.

Chapter Ten

Half the Mice were seriously over-excited and the other half were trembling in their ballet shoes. Lou and Emma, who were supposed to be keeping them in order, were too busy to be either scared or excited.

It was the day of the first performance. The set was in place, the lights had been tested and now, beyond the big closed curtains, the audience could be heard taking their seats.

Everyone backstage wanted to peep round the curtains, but Adrian said it would look 'unprofessional'. Lou agreed; no one at the Opera House had peeped. The red-velvet curtains had kept their secret right up to the wonderful moment

when they had swept back to reveal a complete and magical world. Now it was all about to happen again, she thought, only this time she would be on the other side of the curtain.

Meanwhile, it was her job to calm down half of her Mice and put courage into the others. 'You'll be all right,' she told them firmly. 'You won't see the audience because they're in the dark.'

'And if you do make a mistake, they won't know it's you,' added Emma helpfully, 'because you'll be inside your mouse masks.'

The Rats and Mice looked really convincing. They wore tights and leotards dyed brown and had long tails, which were a bit of a hazard when they were dancing. Sometimes tails got trodden on and there were squeaks of protest. Adrian said this was all right so long as they only squeaked and didn't call each other rude names. He said a bit of squabbling made them more mouse-like. They had been divided into two groups, one led by Lou and one by Emma. This had made it easier to give patterns to their dancing.

The assistant stage manager came round, calling, 'Overture and beginners, please.' This meant that the actors who were on stage first had to get ready in the wings. Lou wished she was one of them, so that she could get that first entrance over.

Miss Ashton came to wish them all good luck, but, as she had explained to them, you must not say 'good luck' in the theatre. Instead she said, 'Break a leg, all of you!' And they chorused, 'Break a leg, Miss Ashton!' in return.

Angela's grandfather came in to see them, looking very splendid in his rich costume. Lou's joke about the Wind-up Merchant had gone all round the company. Adrian said it fitted him

perfectly and even the Merchant seemed to enjoy it.

'There are scouts from the Opera House in the audience,' he said breathlessly. 'It seems they have heard about your Mouse troupe!'

They knew he was teasing, so they just said, 'Yeah . . . yeah,' and told him to break a leg.

One by one their friends vanished on to the stage and then, at last, it was their turn. The stage manager ushered them into the wings; they glimpsed the dim faces of the audience beyond the brightly lit stage; their music began and they were ON!

First they had to show what a nuisance the Mice were by running about the stage with little mouse-like steps, stealing food from the Merchant's table. Each thing they stole had to be carried off-stage and dumped, so that they could run back on and steal something else. This made it look as if there were lots and lots of mice.

It worked very well for the little ones, as their first trip on to the stage was just a quick, scurrying dance and back into the safety of the wings. But it was like going on a scary ride at a fun-fair: when you had plucked up courage and done it once, you couldn't wait to do it again. Soon the little Mice had lost all their stage-fright and would probably have demolished the entire set, if Richard, the Cat, hadn't rushed in and chased them all away.

When the interval came, everyone was full of praise. Miss Ashton said she was proud of them and then gave Lou and

85

Richard a last-minute run-through of their sword fight.

The second act began. Now all the Mice were over-confident, and Lou and Emma had a job keeping them quiet backstage. It was a relief when it was time to go on. This scene was the Court of the African King, so they had all sorts of different food to steal. Sometimes two Mice grabbed the same piece and there were angry tussles. One of the Mice forgot to squeak and shouted, 'Let go! It's mine!' but this just raised a big laugh from beyond the footlights.

The audience was in a really good mood by the time it came to the sword fight. Emma's Rat had been killed and Lou found herself centre stage. For a while she and Richard circled each other,

clashing their wooden swords together.
Then the Cat lunged forward and there
was a gasp from the audience as he ran
the Rat through. Actually the sword thrust
went under Lou's arm, but it looked very
convincing and Lou began her death

stagger. She got rather carried away when she realized that every eye was upon her and the King Rat might have taken a very long time to die. Fortunately, she caught sight of Angela, watching from the middle of the front row. The shock of it finished her off and she fell to the floor. There was a sudden burst of applause from the audience and someone called out, 'Well done, that Rat!' Lying spread-eagled on her back, gazing up into the glare of the stage lights, Lou felt at that moment she could have died happy.

It was probably the best moment of all, but there were still good things to come. At the end of the show there were curtain calls and the Rats and Mice got some of the loudest applause of all. Coming on from the back of the stage, Lou and

Emma each led their little troupe of Mice down to the footlights, where they spread out, joined hands and did their best *révérences* all together. The audience cheered. Then, as Miss Ashton had taught them, they removed their masks and,

holding them in their hands, bowed so
that the audience could see who they
were. Then they put their masks back on
and took their places at the side while the
principal actors came on.

Even after the curtains closed, the
audience went on applauding and they
had to take a second curtain call. As Lou
curtsied for the last time, she stared out
through the eye-holes of her rat mask
and felt that she had come a long way. A
few months back, she had been a skinny
girl in a red bathing suit, practising
curtsies in front of a dingy old mirror.
Now she was a Rat, in full costume,
curtsying to a real audience on a real
stage. One day, she felt quite certain, she
would wear a white embroidered tutu
and a jewelled crown, and make her

graceful *révérence* in front of those magical red and gold curtains on the stage of the Opera House.

Dancing Shoes

Hi!

Emma and I are really glad you like hearing all our news. We thought you'd want to know what we'll be doing next.

Ballet is fantastic! It's lots of fun, but quite hard work. It was so exciting to be in the pantomime – especially playing the Rats!

As you know, we'll soon be leaving the Beginners' Class and joining Angela and the others. We are practising very hard so that we can catch them up. They've been dancing for ages. Luckily Mrs Dillon is helping us by giving us extra coaching after school.

Wish us luck!

Love

Lou

PS Look out for more DANCING SHOES stories coming soon